The Animal Show

Written by Jill Eggleton
Illustrated by Clive Taylor

Guide Notes

Title: The Animal Show
Stage: Emergent – Magenta

Genre: Fiction
Approach: Guided Reading
Processes: Thinking Critically, Exploring Language, Processing Information
Written and Visual Focus: Labels
Word Count: 33

FORMING THE FOUNDATION

Tell the children that the story is about animals in the jungle showing off what they have. Talk to them about what is on the front cover. Read the title and the author / illustrator. 'Walk' through the book focussing on the illustrations and talking to the children about the various animals and what they are showing off.
Talk about the owl and its part in the story. Focus the children's attention on the snake. Leave pages 12-13 for prediction.

Read the text together.

THINKING CRITICALLY
(sample questions)

After the reading
- Why do you think the animals were showing off?
- What do you think might happen if the animals didn't run away from the snake?

EXPLORING LANGUAGE
(ideas for selection)

Terminology
Title, cover, author, illustrator, illustrations

Vocabulary
Interest words: ears, beak, tail, eyes, tongue
High-frequency words: look, at, my, said